MARCUS PFISTER

RAINBOW FISH
TO THE RESCUE

Translated by J. Alison James

NorthSouth
New York / London

A long way out in the deep blue sea, Rainbow Fish swam, ate, and played with his friends. They were so happy together, they had no interest in other fish.

One day a little striped fish swam through the game that Rainbow Fish and his friends were playing.

"Can I play with you?" asked the striped fish.

"It's flash-tag," said one little fish, "and you don't have a flashing scale."

"Do you have to have a special scale?" the little striped fish asked.

"Of course you do!" said the fish with the jagged fins. "Come on, let's play!" he called to the others.

All the fish turned and went back to their game. Rainbow Fish hesitated, but he didn't dare stand up to the fish with the jagged fins. Feeling a little ashamed, Rainbow Fish swam off to join the others.

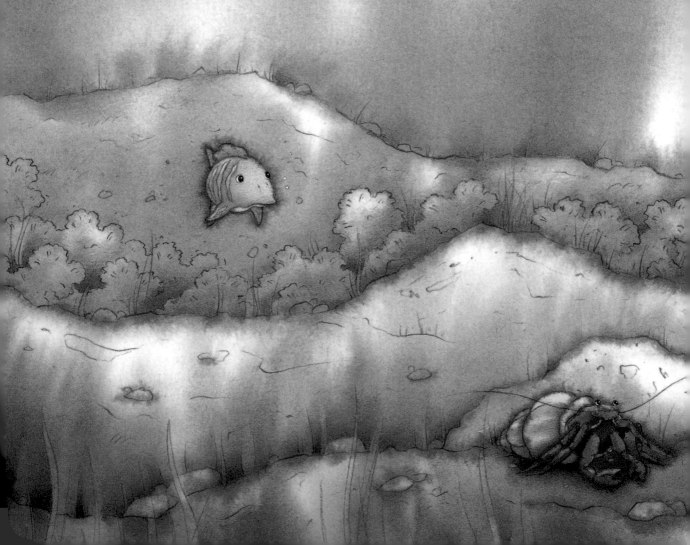

The little striped fish floated all alone at the edge of the reef. He looked sad as he watched the other fish having fun.

Rainbow Fish remembered what it felt like to have no friends. But now he did have friends, and Rainbow Fish soon was caught up in the game.

No one was paying attention when danger entered the reef. . . .

Suddenly a shark shot like an arrow into the middle of the school. The fish darted in every direction and managed to escape to their hiding place.

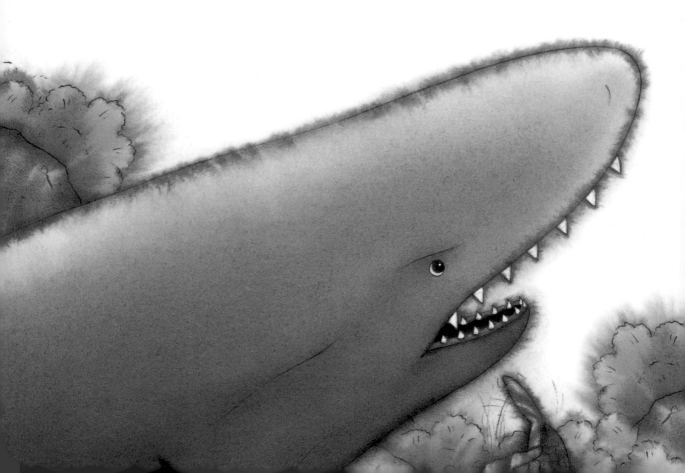

They were safe in a narrow crack in the reef, but the little striped fish wasn't. Rainbow Fish couldn't keep still, he was so worried.

"The little striped fish is all alone out there. We've got to help him!"

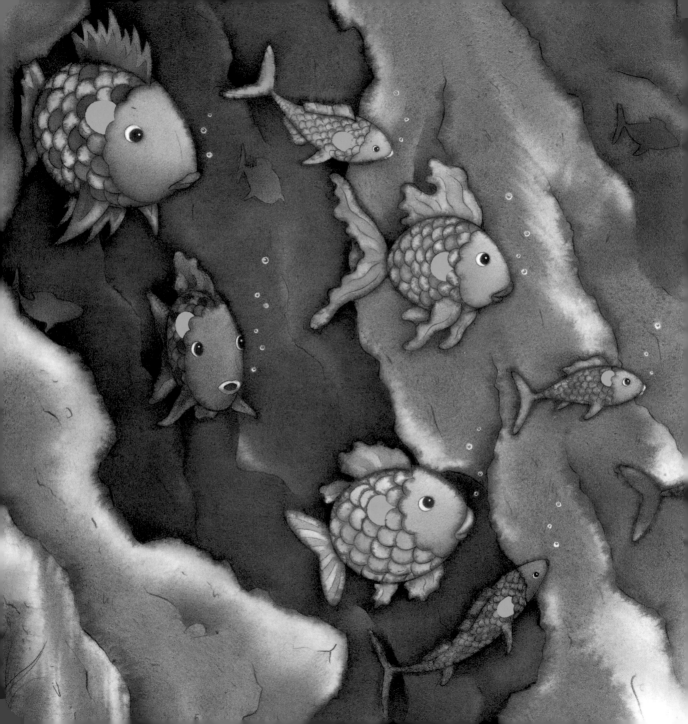

With that, Rainbow Fish left the safety of the hiding place. "Let's go!" he called.

The other fish trembled with fear, but they sped out of the crack after him.

They soon saw the shark and the little
striped fish trying to swim away from his jaws.
"Hurry!" shouted Rainbow Fish, and all the
fish swarmed straight for the shark.
The confused shark turned this way and that,
snapping right and left until he was dizzy. The
shark almost got the fish with the jagged fins,
but he escaped with just a few scratches.

Quietly, Rainbow Fish led the little striped fish to safety as the shark swam away.

"You were really brave," said the little striped fish. "Thanks for saving my life."